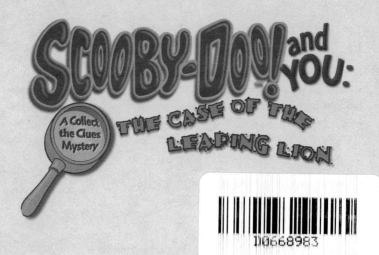

SCOOBY-DOO! and YOU:
A Collect the Clues Mystery
THE CASE OF THE LEAPING LION

By Jenny Markas

WORLDWIDE PUBLISHING™

SCHOLASTIC INC.

New York   Toronto   London   Auckland   Sydney
Mexico City   New Delhi   Hong Kong

For Sophie

ISBN 0-439-23154-X

12 11 10 9 8 7 6 5 4 3 2   1 2 3 4 5/0

Cover and interior illustrations by Duendes del Sur
Cover and interior design by Madalina Stefan

Printed in the U.S.A.

First Scholastic printing, January 2001

"Howdy, pardner!" A waiter in a huge ten-gallon cowboy hat greets you at the door.

"Howdy," you answer. "I'm here to meet some friends —"

Just then, you hear a whoop from across the room. You glance over, and sure enough, there at a corner table are Scooby-Doo and the gang. They're all waving you over.

You grin. "I think I found them," you tell the waiter. You walk over to the table.

1

"Yee-haw!" Shaggy says. "I mean, like, it's great to see you."

Velma hands you a menu. "The burgers here are excellent," she says.

You check the menu, decide on a "Git Along Little Dogie" chili dog with fries, and give the waiter your order.

"Good choice, pardner," he says, beaming.

"Glad you could come," Fred says to you. "We wanted to tell you about our latest mystery."

Your ears perk up. "Another mystery?" you ask. Just then, your chili dog arrives. You pick it up and take a big bite, trying to ignore the fact that both Scooby and Shaggy are watching you hungrily.

"You bet," Fred says. "The Case of the Leaping Lion. It was a tough one, too. But I bet you would have figured it out in no time."

You're flattered. "Really? Tell me more."

"Wait!" Velma says. "Before we tell you all about it, how about if we give you the chance to solve it yourself?"

2

"Great idea," Daphne chimes in. "You can use our Clue Keeper. It's full of information."

"I don't mean to interrupt," Shaggy says, "but, like, are you going to finish that chili dog?"

You look down on your plate and see that the idea of solving a mystery has made you forget all about your lunch. "I guess not," you say, shoving the plate toward Shaggy. He reaches for it, smiling happily.

Shaggy cuts the chili dog in half and pushes the plate toward Scooby. "Take your pick," he says.

Scooby looks over both pieces carefully. Finally, he chooses the one that looks just a teensy bit bigger. He gulps it down in about one second. Shaggy just shakes his head, picks up the other piece, and starts eating.

"Are you two done?" Velma asks, raising an eyebrow.

Both of them nod.

"Then can we go on explaining about the Clue Keeper?" Velma asks.

They nod again.

"How will your Clue Keeper help me solve the mystery?" you ask.

"It's easy," Fred says. "I took all the notes this time. All you have to do is watch for this sign 👁👁." He opens the Clue Keeper to show you. "When you see that, you'll know you're meeting a suspect." Then he points to another symbol. "And when you see this 🔑, you'll know you've found a clue."

"We'll help you organize your thinking with some questions at the end of each Clue Keeper section," Velma adds.

"And that's it!" Daphne says. "Put it all together, and you'll be able to solve the mystery just like we did."

"Are you going to finish those onion rings?" Shaggy asks Fred. But you hardly even notice. Fred hands you the Clue Keeper and you're on your way to solving *The Case of the Leaping Lion.*

Clue Keeper Entry 1

"Where are the giraffes? I love giraffes." Velma was checking the big map.

"And the orangutans?" Shaggy adds. "Where are those?"

A man in a tan safari suit held up his hands. "Don't worry," he said. "You can see it all. There's plenty of time. I'm so glad you came to visit the Centerville Zoo!"

I looked around. I saw clean cages, well

kept buildings, lots of pretty plants, and winding, litter-free walkways.

"This is a nice zoo," I said. "Not too big, not too small. Plenty to see. It looks like you have a wonderful place here."

The man sighed. "Thanks. I think so, too. This zoo has been in my family for three generations. I'm Karl Underhill, and my grandfather Jonah started this zoo when he first came to this country. At that time he only

had a few monkeys, an elephant, and a couple of rare birds."

"You have a lot more than that now," I said. "According to your map, you have everything from ring-tailed lemurs to crocodiles to penguins."

He sighed again. "That's true," he said. "We do have plenty of animals. But, unfortunately, we lack people. We're not getting as many customers as we used to, so money is short."

"Where did the customers go?" Daphne asked.

Karl Underhill shrugged. "I'm not sure," he said, without meeting our eyes. "Some strange things have happened recently. It's been tough. People are scared to come here. I've even had to sell some of my animals just to make the money to keep the zoo open. People have heard the rumors."

"What rumors?" I asked.

"I'd rather not say," Mr. Underhill told us. "Something has been happening, but I don't even want to talk about it. It's too bizarre. I'm not even sure it's real. Maybe it's just that everybody would rather go to the movies, or check out the rides at an amusement park."

"Or play with their computers," put in another man, short and round and wearing a business suit. He had come up beside Karl Underhill and was carrying a huge, oversized briefcase. Two other men, in similar suits, stood near him. "Computers are

where it's at. You can do anything with computers."

"You can't have a zoo," Velma pointed out.

"Aha!" The man stuck a finger into the air. "That's where you're wrong." He pulled out a business card and handed it to her. "Harold Pointer, at your service."

Velma looked at the card. "Virtual Visions?" she asked. "What kind of business is that?"

"A growing one!" Harold Pointer said, beaming. "My colleagues and I," he gestured to the two men, "make dreams come true. We can make anything you imagine into reality. Well, into virtual reality, that is."

"I've heard of virtual reality," I said. "That's where computer technology makes you feel as if you're really doing something, when you're not. Like flying a rocketship, or playing football. But how can you have a virtual zoo?"

"Easy," Harold Pointer proclaimed. "Virtual Visions can do it. And we *will* do it, as soon as we find the right place." He looked around. "Something like . . . this," he said.

"We can use the same cages, the same walkways, the same everything. People can come and see the animals, just like they do now. But here's the beauty of it: the animals won't be real. They won't need to eat, or sleep. They won't get sick. Their cages won't have to be cleaned. They'll be *virtual* animals — animal images we project into their habitats."

"Never!" Karl Underhill crossed his arms. "I'll never let you do that to my zoo. The only animal worth seeing is a real animal — an animal that breathes and lives. Call me old-fashioned, but that's the way I feel."

Harold Pointer shrugged. "Whatever," he said. "I'm patient."

"You'll have to be," Karl Underhill said. "Because it'll never happen. Not as long as I own this zoo."

Harold Pointer just smiled and strolled off. His buddies followed close behind him.

"Nice to meet you, too," Daphne called after him. She turned to Karl Underhill. "I don't blame you for not wanting to sell your zoo to him. What an idea!"

"I wouldn't want to see virtual giraffes," Velma added, shaking her head. "Only real ones."

"Well," Karl Underhill said, smiling, "I just happen to have a few of those. Shall we go see them?"

"I can't wait to see the giraffes. But before we get there, maybe we should take the time to answer a few questions. I bet you saw the in this Clue Keeper entry. That means we've met a suspect! See if you can answer the following questions."

1. What is the suspect's name?

2. What does he do for a living?

3. Why would he be interested in the Centerville Zoo going out of business?

13

Clue Keeper Entry 2

"Zoinks!" Shaggy stared. "Would you look at those necks?"

Karl had led us to the giraffes, then excused himself. "I need to check on the baboons," he said. "I'll be back in a few minutes."

The giraffes moved slowly by, walking with surprisingly graceful motions. Their heads floated high above us as they strolled around their enclosure.

"Their long necks allow them to eat the most tender leaves from the treetops," said a thin, blond woman standing nearby. She was wearing a flowered dress and a big straw hat, and she carried a matching straw

bag. "At least, when they're in the wild. Here they just get fed by the zookeepers."

She sounded like she knew a lot about animals. She also sounded a little upset.

"I'm sure the zookeepers take good care of them," I said.

"That's not the point," said the woman. "I should introduce myself. My name is July Summers, and I belong to a group called Free the Animals." The woman reached into her bag and pulled out a stack of pamphlets. She handed one to each of us, including Scooby.

"Ranks," said Scooby, looking a little bewildered.

I looked at the pamphlet. "Zoos are unfair to animals," it said. "Animals belong in their natural habitats, not in cages."

"But zoos are great for children," Daphne pointed out. "How else could they see things like giraffes and hippos?"

The woman shook her head. "They can see them on TV, or in books. Animals should not be held captive just for our entertainment."

"But wouldn't they have trouble learning to survive in the wild?" Velma asked. "After all, they've spent most of their time in the zoo, being cared for by people."

July Summers nodded. "That's very true. But my group has ways of helping animals learn to cope in the wild." She reached over to show me a section of the pamphlet that explained the group's program.

"Not you again!" We looked up from our pamphlets to see Karl Underhill approaching. "Do you really have to hand out those pamphlets at my zoo? This is a good zoo. We take good care of our animals."

July Summers didn't back down. "No zoo is a good zoo." She closed up her bag and said good-bye. "I'm off to see the tigers," she said. "They miss me if I don't stop by every day."

We watched her walk off. Karl Underhill shook his head. "She's a nice lady," he said. "But she and her group just don't understand. They'd like to put me — and every other zookeeper around — out of business."

"She seems to know all about the animals," I said. *And she sure would like to see this zoo closed,* I thought.

Shaggy sniffed. "Hey, not to change the subject or anything, but do I smell popcorn?" he asked.

Karl Underhill smiled. "I bet you do," he said. "There's a stand nearby. Shall we go find it?"

Scooby nodded eagerly. *"Ropcorn!"* he said.

"Lead the way," Shaggy said.

As we headed down a path, I wondered how we could get Mr. Underhill to tell us what strange things had been happening at the zoo.

"How about those giraffes? Pretty cool. Maybe you also noticed that we met another suspect in the last Clue Keeper entry. If so, can you answer the following questions?"

1. What is the suspect's name?

2. What group does the suspect belong to?

3. Why would the suspect want to close down the Centerville Zoo?

"Now, let's go join Shaggy and Scooby for some popcorn. And maybe after that, I'll finally get to see my hippos."

Clue Keeper Entry 3

"Mmm, that looks awesome," Shaggy said as we approached the popcorn cart. "I'll take a Jumbo Supreme, please," he told the man running the cart.

He put down the large bag he was holding and showed Shaggy a much, much larger one. "Yeah, that's good," Shaggy agreed.

"Excellent," the man said. "That'll be plenty for you and your friends."

"I don't know about my friends," Shaggy said. "Like, they can order whatever size they want. This one's just for me."

Scooby frowned and tugged at Shaggy's sleeve.

"Oops," Shaggy said. "Me and Scooby, that is."

"There you go," the man said, handing Shaggy the bucket. Then the rest of us ordered. I was just getting my popcorn when I noticed Karl Underhill talking to a tall red-haired man nearby.

"Not today. Not tomorrow. And, if I have my way, *never*," Karl was saying. "I'll never sell you my ring-tailed lemur."

"Just asking," the man answered, shrugging his shoulders. "I know you were happy to sell me those koala bears last week."

"I wasn't happy. I wasn't happy about that at all. But I needed the money." Karl Underhill looked sad.

I remembered Karl telling us that he'd

had to sell several animals just to make ends meet. This must be the man he'd sold them to. He called us over and introduced us.

"Kids, this is Morley Blanks," he told us.

"Nice to meet you, kids," the man said. "Are you enjoying your day at the zoo?"

"Abzhorootly," Shaggy said, through a mouthful of popcorn. He swallowed. "I mean, absolutely. This place is excellent!"

"I agree," Morley Blanks said. "That's why I do what I can to make sure it stays open."

"Ha!" Karl Underhill said. "You mean, by buying up my animals one by one and selling them to other zoos — at three times the price you paid — you think you're actually *helping* me?"

"Sure," Morley Blanks said. "If you hadn't sold me those animals, would you have had enough money to stay open this long?"

Karl looked down at his shoes. "Nope," he said. "I guess not. But how much longer can I stay open if I have to sell off all my animals?"

Morley Blanks shrugged. "That's your problem," he said as he walked away.

The rest of us stood there, eating popcorn and thinking over the problem.

"Maybe if you could get more people to come here, you'd be able to keep the zoo open without selling animals," Daphne sug-gested.

Karl sighed. "I've tried," he said. "I've done everything I can to draw crowds. But something always happens to drive the people away."

"Like, what could happen at a zoo?" Shaggy asked. "A zoo is a happy, peaceful place. What could drive people away from a zoo?"

Just then, we all heard a tremendous roar. And a crowd of people ran by.

"Like, that popcorn was the best! Drenched with butter, lightly sprinkled with salt, each tender kernel popped to, like, perfection . . . It was, like – oops! I guess I'm supposed to be asking you some questions about the suspect you met in this Clue Keeper Entry. Like, here they are."

1. What is the suspect's name?

2. What does he do for a living?

3. Why would he be interested in the Centerville Zoo closing down?

Clue Keeper Entry 4

"*O*h, no!" Karl said. "Not again!" He checked his watch. "And so near feeding time." He looked very upset.

I gave him a curious look. "What's going on?" I asked.

"This is the thing I didn't want to tell you about, because you would have been scared off like everybody else," Karl confessed.

We heard another roar.

"Help! Help!" People were running by us now. "The lion is out of its cage!"

Karl shook his head. "It's not *my* lion," he said helplessly. "If it were, I would know how to deal with it."

"What do you mean?" Daphne asked. "Where else would a lion come from?"

Karl shrugged. "I don't know. I've been trying to figure that out. We call it the Leaping Lion because of the way it runs. It appears whenever there are the most people in the zoo. We try to catch it, but we can't. Eventually, it just disappears. And after its visits, other things always go wrong. Once the penguins were let out of their enclosure. Another time the rhinoceros was found in the camel pen."

There was another roar.

"There's no time to talk about it now!" I shouted.

"Like, it's coming this way!" Shaggy yelled.

We waited to see what the Leaping Lion looked like. I'm not sure if that was a good

idea. I think it might give us nightmares for a while.

Why?

Because this was no ordinary lion. It was bigger, scarier, and more ferocious than any lion I'd ever seen. Its red mouth opened wider than you could imagine with every roar, and its teeth were gigantic. Its mane was like a huge cloud around its neck.

The Leaping Lion came toward us, chas-

ing the people along a twisty path past the monkey house and the polar bear habitat. A peacock that was strolling along, free because it has no wings to fly away, jumped and hid in the bushes. The Leaping Lion chased it for a moment, running right through a pond with a fountain without even seeming to notice the water.

The roars were ear-splitting as the Leaping Lion passed us by.

"The Leaping Lion has never hurt anyone," Karl told us. "But it sure scares a lot of people."

"That Leaping Lion is no regular feline," I said, looking down at the path it had just run along. "This mystery needs to be cleared up fast if the zoo is going to stay open."

"Well, then, we're on the case!" Velma said.

"You bet," I said. "What do you say, gang? Time to split up and look for clues?"

"Definitely," Velma said. "I'll go with Shaggy and Scooby. You and Daphne can check the north end of the zoo, and we'll check the south. Let's meet up by the snack bar to exchange information."

"Sounds like a plan!" I said.

Just then, an assistant zookeeper in green pants and a green shirt ran up to Karl. His nametag read TOM.

"Mr. Underhill!" he said. "Something strange is going on."

"What, Tom?" Karl asked. "What is it now?"

"Well, sir," he said, stepping closer. "All the animals are asleep!"

30

Clue Keeper Entry 5

"Asleep?" Karl Underhill asked. "What do you mean?"

"Just what I said," the man told him. "Every single animal in the zoo is snoozing. The monkeys, the seals, even the baby gnus!"

"It's just like you were telling us," I said.

"After the Leaping Lion shows up, strange things happen."

"I'd better check on my animals," Karl said. "And we'll try to catch that Leaping Lion, too, even though we never do. It's probably disappeared by now, anyway."

He gave the assistant zookeeper some directions. Meanwhile, Daphne and I headed up the path toward the elephant house, while Velma set off with Shaggy and Scooby.

The zoo seemed very, very quiet all of a sudden. And it wasn't just that the Leaping Lion had stopped roaring. The fact was, not one of the animals was making a sound. A silent zoo.

"Strange, isn't it?" I asked.

"It sure is," Daphne said. "Look!" She pointed into the enclosure where the chimpanzees live. They were all fast asleep. Baby chimpanzees were sleeping soundly next to their mothers. The biggest chimpanzees were draped over tree limbs, snoozing away, way up high.

A little way up the path, we passed by the

water buffalo enclosure. The big animals were still on their feet, but their heads hung down. They were obviously napping.

"I know lots of animals sleep during the day," I said. "But this is crazy. How could all the animals be asleep at the same time?"

By then we had come to the elephant house. We looked inside, and sure enough, the elephants were snoozing, too. Some of them were sleeping standing up, like the water buffalo, and some were on their sides.

A particularly huge elephant had fallen asleep, leaning against a tree. I wondered how long the tree could stay standing. The elephant must have been eating right before he fell asleep because he was still clutching a big wad of hay in his trunk. It was as if he'd fallen asleep right in the middle of eating.

That made me stop and think.

"Daphne, that's it!" I said. "Somebody must have put something in the animals' food."

"You're right," she replied. "And maybe this is what it was in."

She knelt and picked up a small brown bottle with a dropper in the spout.

The words on the label were scratched out, but Daphne was able to read a little of the remaining writing. "Give two drops at bedtime to insure a good night's . . ."

That was all she could read, but it sure sounded like some kind of sleeping medication to me.

"That's got to be what happened," I said.

"Karl Underhill said it was feeding time. Somebody must have put that sleeping medicine in all the food. They did it when the Leaping Lion was running through the zoo, distracting everyone. The animals ate it, and now they're all asleep."

Daphne nodded. "I bet you're right," she said. "And it's just the kind of thing someone might do if they want to see the zoo be shut down. After all, how many people are going to pay to see a bunch of snoozing animals?"

"Excellent point, my dear." We turned to see Harold Pointer standing nearby. He was still carrying that huge briefcase. I didn't see his two friends around, though. "And just think, with a virtual zoo, the animals would *never* have to sleep."

Just then, the elephant leaning against the tree opened one eye. Suddenly, the zoo was coming back to life.

"**D**id you ever hear of such a thing? Naptime at the zoo. We never saw so many sleeping animals at once before. Oh, well, naptime's over. But meanwhile, did you catch the ⚷ ? That means you've found a clue. Answer the following questions and you'll be on your way to solving this mystery."

1. What clue did you find in this entry?

2. Why do you think this clue is important?

3. Which of the suspects might be responsible for this clue?

37

Clue Keeper Entry 6

Meanwhile, Velma was looking all over with Shaggy and Scooby. She told me later that, as they walked along the paths, the zoo seemed very, very quiet. When she turned to speak to Scooby and Shaggy, they were gone. "Shaggy!" she called. "Scooby! Scooby-Doo, where are you?"

Suddenly, a head popped up from between a couple of decorative shrubs. It was Shaggy! Scooby's head popped up, too.

"Were you hiding from the Leaping Lion?" Velma folded her arms and gave Shaggy a look.

"Leaping Lion? Hiding? No way! Not us!" Shaggy insisted. He looked around nervously.

Shaggy and Scooby jumped out of the bushes. "Like, let's start looking for clues."

The three of them started walking down the path, past the penguins. The penguins had been asleep, like all the other animals, but by then they were starting to wake up. They waddled around, some of them slipping into the water and swimming along as Shaggy, Scooby, and Velma walked past their pool.

Shaggy laughed. "I love those little guys," he said. "They're the coolest." He waved at the penguins. "Too bad they have to live on raw fish," he went on, shuddering. "I can eat a lot of things, but I couldn't eat that. No way."

"*Ro ray,*" Scooby agreed, shaking his head.

"I'm with you two," Velma said, laughing.

As they passed the enclosure that held the ostriches, they heard an assistant zookeeper speaking into his walkie-talkie. "I'm telling you, it's gone. Kaput. Disappeared."

"Is he talking about the Leaping Lion?" Shaggy asked. "Like, that would be good news."

The man clicked off his radio and glared at Shaggy. He was dressed all in green, and his name tag read ZEKE. "I'm not talking about the Leaping Lion," he answered. "He's gone, too. But that's not what I'm worried about. It's the sloth. The giant three-toed sloth. He's missing!"

"How can that be?" Velma asked.

Zeke shrugged. "Things happen around here when that Leaping Lion appears. Strange things."

"We'll help you find him," Velma offered.

"Like, how do you find a three-toed sloth?" Shaggy asked, scratching his head. "Where do they like to hang out?"

"In trees, mostly," Zeke answered. "But I don't think this one walked away on his own. I think he was stolen." He led Shaggy, Velma, and Scooby over to a cage. "See?" He pointed to the ground. "Tire tracks."

"So let's follow the tracks, and maybe we'll find the sloth!" Velma suggested. The four of them started running, following the tracks along the path until they came to the zoo gates.

On the way, they passed Morley Blanks. He was standing near the ring-tailed lemur cage, looking wistfully at the furry animal inside. He didn't even seem to notice as the group ran by.

Just outside the gates was a big van with its windows blacked out. It was parked beneath a tree, with no driver in sight. But Velma spotted something. A tuft of fur was caught in the door. "Check out that van!" she cried. Zeke hurried over and flung open the doors. Sure enough, a huge, furry animal was inside.

"The sloth!" Zeke cried. He pulled out his radio and called for help. "We found him! Come help me bring him back to his cage!"

"Wow, that was close," Shaggy said. "Somebody was trying to steal the sloth. But why would someone do that?"

"Good question," Velma answered. "I think it's time to meet up with Fred and Daphne at the snack bar. Maybe they've found some clues, too. Hopefully we can put everything together and solve this mystery!"

"Snack bar, here we come!" Shaggy said happily. "I just hope they're not serving raw fish today!"

43

"Good thing we found that sloth! I think he'll be happier back in his cage at the zoo, where everything's just the way he likes it. The clue you found in this chapter helped us find the sloth, but it should also help you solve the mystery. Answer the following questions, if you can."

1. What clue did you find in this entry?

2. Why do you think this clue is important?

3. Which of the suspects might be responsible for this clue?

44

Clue Keeper Entry 7

Velma, Shaggy, and Scooby set out for the snack bar. They paused for a moment to watch the penguins' antics one more time.

"Adorable, aren't they?" July Summers was watching, too. "And to think they're stuck here in a zoo. They belong down in Antarctica, where they came from, in a land of snow and ice and cold, cold water. . . ."

She went on for a while about Antarctica. From the way she made it sound, Shaggy couldn't help thinking that the penguins were better off here in the Centerville Zoo.

As they watched, a delicious smell wafted over. Scooby's nose twitched. So did Shaggy's. "What's that I smell?" Shaggy asked. "I think — no, I'm sure of it! It's cotton candy!"

"Mmm!" Scooby said, rubbing his tummy.

"I've got to have some, now!" Shaggy said.

"Shaggy," Velma protested, "we're on our way to the snack bar. You can get something to eat there."

"But they might not have cotton candy!" Shaggy pointed out. "And, like, once I smell that stuff, I have to have some."

"Oh, all right," Velma said. "You go ahead and find it. I'll meet you at the snack bar. But Shaggy, be careful!"

"Careful?" asked Shaggy. "Why? What could happen? The Leaping Lion is gone, the sloth is heading back to its cage. Everything is fine." He grinned at Velma. "Don't worry. We'll be there as soon as we get our cotton candy."

46

He and Scooby zoomed off in the direction the smell was coming from, and Velma headed on over to the snack bar to meet me and Daphne.

"There you are!" I said, when I saw her. "Have you found any clues? And where are Scooby and Shaggy?"

She explained about the cotton candy. Then she told us about the missing sloth. "We helped to find it, but we never did figure out who was trying to steal it."

Then Daphne and I told her about somebody putting sleeping medicine into the animals' food. "Sounds like the same person might be responsible," I said. "And whoever it is must be connected somehow with that Leaping Lion, since he always appears just before strange things happen."

"Speaking of strange things," Daphne said, "do you hear what I hear?"

We listened for a second. I heard the sound of a distant roar. Then it got closer. I looked at Daphne and Velma, and we all gulped. "The Leaping Lion!" I said. "It's here again, and it's getting closer!"

Just then, Shaggy and Scooby came into view. They were running as fast as they could, trailing clouds of pink cotton candy behind them.

The Leaping Lion's roars grew louder, much louder. Then we saw him. He was following right behind Shaggy and Scooby, bounding along with his huge, scary mouth wide open. I could see every tooth, and believe me, they were gigantic.

"Save us! Save us!" yelled Shaggy as he ran past. He splashed through a little stream as he took a shortcut toward us. The Leaping Lion splashed right behind him.

"Over here!" I cried, gesturing toward a gate leading into the snack bar's eating area.

Shaggy took a quick turn into the garden. Scooby followed him, screeching to a halt as soon as they were safely inside. They both watched, cowering behind a bush, as the Leaping Lion bounded past.

"Like, whew!" Shaggy said. "That was close." He looked down at his hand, and his face fell. "Oh, man. I lost all my cotton candy!"

"Don't worry about your cotton candy," I told him. "There's plenty to eat here. The main thing is that you're safe."

Then Daphne spoke up. "You know what?" she asked. "I think they were safe all along."

"What?" Velma and I turned to stare at her.

"I don't think that's a real lion," Daphne said.

"Really?" Shaggy looked relieved. "But, like, how can you tell?"

"Because he didn't leave any tracks." Daphne pointed to the ground. "Look, you and Scooby left wet tracks behind you because you had just run through the stream. The Leaping Lion went through the stream, too. But where are his tracks?"

We all stared at the ground. "That's it!" I said, slapping my forehead. "I knew there was something strange about that lion before. It was the same thing! He didn't leave any tracks on the path after he ran through the fountain!"

"This Leaping Lion is somebody's creation," Daphne said.

"I think you're right," I agreed. "Now all we have to do is figure out whose."

Daphne's Mystery-Solving Tips

"Wow, that was a close call! Or at least, it seemed that way at the time. But Shaggy and Scooby are safe. In fact, I think they're eating onion rings right now, over at the snack bar. While they eat, can you answer the following questions?"

 1. What clue did you find in this entry?

2. Why do you think this clue is important?

 3. Which of the suspects might be responsible for this clue?

52

Clue Keeper Entry 8

"If we could just see that Leaping Lion one more time, I bet we could figure out the truth about it," I said.

"But, like, how can we get the Leaping Lion to make an appearance?" Shaggy asked.

"I know!" Daphne spoke up. "If Shaggy

and Scooby dressed up like zookeepers, the Leaping Lion might come to chase them."

"Ro ray!" Scooby said, shaking his head.

"Scooby's right," Shaggy agreed. "No way. That sounds way too dangerous."

"Come on," Velma pleaded. "It's the only way. Don't you want to save the zoo?"

"Well . . ." Shaggy looked down at his feet.

"Scooby, would you do it for a Scooby Snack?" Daphne asked.

Scooby frowned and shook his head. *"Rope,"* he said, crossing his arms.

"That Leaping Lion *is* pretty scary," I said. "How about for two Scooby Snacks?"

Scooby's frown disappeared.

"Two Scooby Snacks — and we'll make sure you both get all the cotton candy you can eat!" Daphne promised.

"You're on!" Shaggy cried.

"Rokay," Scooby agreed.

Daphne pulled out two Scooby Snacks and threw them up into the air, one at a time. Scooby snapped them up and gobbled them down.

"Like, where's my cotton candy?" Shaggy asked.

"You'll get it," I told him. "But first, put this on." I held out a green uniform, just like the ones the other assistant zookeepers were wearing.

The name tag read DEXTER.

Scooby's uniform had a name tag that read JUNIOR.

The two of them looked just perfect once they'd put the uniforms on. "I bet that Leaping Lion will appear as soon as you start cleaning the elephant house," I told them.

"Cleaning *what*?" Shaggy asked. "You didn't mention that part."

"Oops," I said. "Sorry!"

Grumbling, Shaggy and Scooby picked up shovels and rakes and started to push a wheelbarrow toward the elephant house. The rest of us followed along behind.

"When the Leaping Lion appears," I told the others, "you two keep a close eye on it. I'll be checking around nearby, trying to figure out where it came from."

"Deal," Velma said.

Just then, we all heard a tremendous roaring sound. Shaggy stopped in his tracks, dropped his shovels, and started to run. Scooby was right behind him.

And the Leaping Lion was right behind both of them. He looked bigger than ever, and his mouth was open wide as he roared his loudest.

"Save us!" yelled Shaggy.

Velma and Daphne watched the Leaping Lion carefully. But I looked in the other direction. And sure enough, I saw something that made me suspicious. Everybody else was running away from the Leaping Lion. But one person was following *behind* the Leaping Lion.

"Hey," I said. "What do you think you're doing?"

The person looked at me.

Then the person dropped something big, turned, and ran away — right into the grasp of the security guard I had signaled to!

The second the person was gone, the Leaping Lion was, too.

"It went all fuzzy," Daphne said, when I rejoined the others. "And then it just disappeared."

"I'm not surprised," I said. "Because, in a way, you could say the Leaping Lion was right in here." I held up the object that the person had dropped.

The gang looks at you, smiling. "So?" Fred asks. "Any idea what I was holding?"

"And can you guess who it was that got grabbed by the security guard?" Daphne asks.

"And are you going to finish those fries?" Shaggy asks. "Because, if you're not . . ."

You tell him to go for it. "I can't eat a thing," you say, "until I solve this mystery."

Scooby's eyes light up as Shaggy starts putting ketchup on the fries.

"We can give you a little help," Velma

says. "The first thing to do is to think about your suspects. Which of them had a good reason to scare customers away from the Centerville Zoo?"

"Next," Daphne says, "think about which of them might have left the clues we found."

"If you can," Fred adds, "you should try to eliminate some of the suspects."

You're thinking hard. This is a tough mystery!

"Look over your Clue Keeper carefully," Fred says. "Then, when you're ready, you can guess where that Leaping Lion came from. We'll tell you if you're right!

Turn the page to find out if you've solved The Case of the Leaping Lion correctly.

"It was a virtual lion!" Daphne exclaims. "Did you guess?"

"Harold Pointer created it. He was the one I saw following *behind* the Leaping Lion," Fred says. "And the technology for making that lion image was all inside his huge brief-case. That was the object he dropped."

"He was trying to force Karl Underhill to sell the zoo," Velma adds. "If the zoo didn't attract and keep more customers, Karl would have to sell. So he made the zoo a scary place to visit by creating the lion image. While the lion was scaring people off, Pointer's helpers pulled other pranks guaranteed to drive away customers, like putting all the animals to sleep, or stealing the sloth. Once he owned the zoo, Pointer was planning to sell all the animals to Morley Blanks, and start over with a virtual zoo."

"At first we thought Morely Blanks might be the one who was causing all the strange things to happen, Fred says. "But Morely Blanks didn't have the capability to create that lion image."

"I was suspicious of July Summers," Velma adds. "But she was harmless. She just didn't believe animals should be in zoos."

"So, did you guess right?" Daphne asks.

"If not, don't worry. This was a tough case," Fred tells you.

Daphne signals to a waiter in a cowboy hat, who trundles over a whole wheelbarrow piled high with cotton candy.

"Surprise!" the gang yells.

"Zoinks!" Shaggy's eyes grow round as he stares at the pile of cotton candy.

"Roinks!" Scooby echoes.

Then they both dive in. The pink fluff soon covers their faces. All you can see is their smiles.

"Rooby-rooby-roo!" yells Scooby, as he takes another huge bite.